DRUM STICKS

Matt has a bus to catch.
He is off to test a drum kit.

Matt has a big bag.
He packs his drum sticks
in a thick sock.

"This is a long quest," grins Matt. "I must pack a lot of snacks."

Liz and Matt chat at the bus stop. Matt's back pack is on the bench.

Matt gets on the bus.
His sock is not in his bag!

"Quick! Stop the bus!"
yells Liz. "I have the
drum sticks!"

JUMPING JACK GAME

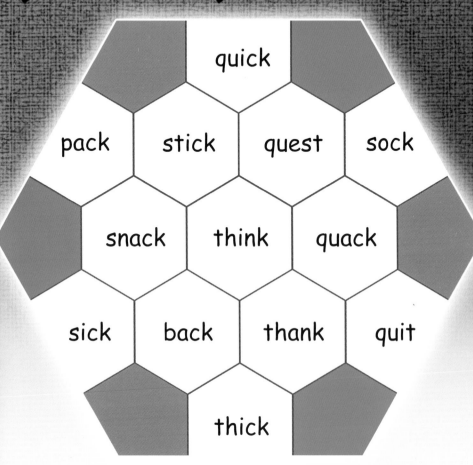

This is a game for two players. Each player has three counters, each set a different color. Players choose to be Red or Blue and place one counter on each of their colors. Players take turns to move a counter by sliding it into an adjacent space or by jumping over their opponent's counter into an empty space. When a player lands on a word, he/she must read the word aloud. The winner is the first player to get all three of his/her counters in a straight line.